MOLEHOLE MYSTERIES

DUSTY MOLE PRIVATE EYE

WRITTEN BY
Barbara Davoll
Pictures by Dennis Hockerman

MOODY PRESS
CHICAGO

Moody Press, a ministry of the Moody Bible Institute,
is designed for education, evangelization, and edifi-
cation. If we may assist you in knowing more about
Christ and the Christian life, please write us without
obligation: Moody Press, c/o MLM, Chicago, IL 60610.
Printed in MEXICO.

ISBN: 0-8024-2700-6

Children love the stories of Barbara Davoll, known for her award-winning, best-selling Christopher Churchmouse Classics and now for the Molehole Mystery series. Barbara writes these zany new adventures in Schroon Lake, New York where she and her husband, Roy, minister at home and abroad with Word of Life International in their Missions Department, Barb manages to stay busy as a wife, mother, grandmother, author, drama teacher, church musician, and homemaker for her husband and Josh, the family Schnauzer.

Illustrator Dennis Hockerman has concentrated on art for children's trade books and textbooks, magazines, greeting cards, and games. He lives with his wife and three children in Mequon, Wisconsin, a suburb of Milwaukee. Mr. Hockerman probably spent more time "underground" than above while developing the characters and creating the etchings for the Molehole Mysteries. Periodically, he would poke his head into his "upstairs connection" to join his family and share with them the adventures of his friends in Molesbury R.F.D.

Contents

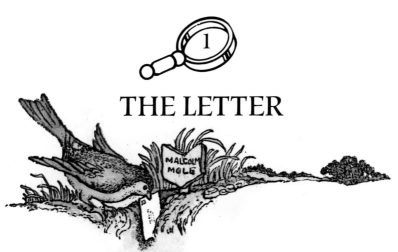

THE LETTER

Just to the left of the old hollow tree where Reuben Robin usually sings his morning concert is a sign pointing the way to Molesbury R. F. D. If you look closely you might see a winding dusty trail. The trail leads down under the ground to the village of Molesbury. A large family of moles lives in this underground home in happy harmony.

One fine summer day there was a growing excitement in the air. Earlier that morning Reuben Robin had delivered a mysterious airmail letter to Malcolm

Mole. All the moles in this little underground village were anxiously waiting to hear what important news was in that letter. Perhaps the letter was some word from the town's leading citizen, Murky Mole, who had disappeared from Molesbury a few weeks ago.

Inside the burrow of Malcolm Mole there was excitement too. Mrs. Miranda Mole and the twins, Dusty and Musty, were anxiously waiting as their father, Malcolm, read the letter. They were certain the letter must be from their Uncle Murky.

"Is the letter from Uncle Murky?" asked Musty, the little girl mole.

"What does he say, dear?" asked Mrs. Miranda, who had laid aside her mending to watch her husband. "Is Murky all right?"

"Umm, yes," murmured Malcolm, not looking up. At last he lowered the letter and peered at them over his glasses. "He's working for the police as an underground agent and can't tell us where he is."

"The Underground?" gasped Mrs. Miranda. "Isn't that extremely dangerous?"

"Oh, wow!" exclaimed Dusty. "I'll say. The Underground! No wonder we haven't heard from him!"

"He isn't coming home—at least not for now," replied Malcolm thoughtfully. "He won't come back to Molesbury until he finishes his job with the police Upstairs." The moles always called the ground above "Upstairs." They didn't go up there often because they didn't see well above ground.

It was just like Uncle
Murky to do something
dangerous like this, Dusty
thought. His uncle was from
a fine family of Murky
Moles who were always
helping others and
doing rescue work.

Malcolm
picked up the
letter again and studied it
a bit more. "He would like our Dusty to join him as a
junior agent in his work. It seems he needs a smaller
mole who can get in and out of small areas easily."

"What?" gasped the mother mole. "Why that is
unthinkable! Dusty is—"

"—is growing up, my dear," interrupted her husband,
"and will soon be on his own. This will be a good way
for him to learn, Miranda. It will teach him responsibility."

"Oh, Father, may I go too?" squealed Musty excitedly.
"I could help Dusty so he won't lose his glasses. I could
wash his clothes and cook for him and Uncle Murky.
Please say I may go, Father," she begged.

Dusty looked at his sister with disgust. "Aw, come on, Musty. This is no job for a girl. I may lose my glasses—but you'd lose yourself. You know you can't find your way out of a paper bag without a map."

"I can too," said Musty with a stamp of her foot. "You take that back, Dusty. I can always find you because you leave such a cloud of dust behind you."

"I'm afraid your father is right, dear," replied her mother. "If Dusty has to go, I suppose he must. But you stay home with me."

Dusty could not believe it. He was going to work with his Uncle Murky. Why, he would be another Squirrelock Holmes. He had always admired the great squirrel detective so much and had read every one of the mystery stories about him. He scurried off to find his mystery books. He wanted to read up on some of Squirrelock's techniques. It was an important job, becoming a junior agent.

Mrs. Miranda Mole dabbed her eyes with her hanky and said tearfully, "I will worry so about my son in such a dangerous business."

"Don't worry, Mother," said Malcolm. "Reuben Robin will watch over him. He has a special radar sense and can keep in touch with us by airmail."

Musty stood quietly thinking as her parents talked. She was not going to be left behind if she could help it. She had to figure out a way to go along.

PRIVATE EYE

Musty headed toward her own cozy room lined with soft earth to think about Dusty's trip and how she might go along. As she passed the doorway of his room she saw that he was making something with his paint box and brushes. Stepping inside she saw it was a sign that read "Dusty Mole, Private Eye."

"Whatcha gonna do with that, Dusty?" she inquired. "Are you taking that with you?"

"Sure," answered Dusty. "I thought I might need it if I set up my detective practice before I return here. Then folks will know what I do." Sometimes Dusty was a little proud and wanted everyone to know how important he was.

"Wouldn't it be better to say junior agent?" asked Musty. "You really aren't a private eye yet."

"Naw, private eye is OK. That's what I want it to say," he insisted. "I guess all my friends will be wishing they could go too. But, of course, not everyone can be a private eye," he added proudly.

"Oh, pooh! Any mole could do that if he weren't too big. Uncle Murky needs you because you're small and—"

"And tough," interrupted her brother. "You gotta be tough to be a private eye, Musty."

That evening the citizens of Molesbury gave a grand party at the Town Hall for Dusty. After a long speech by the mayor, they gave Dusty some useful gifts to take with him. The gift he liked best was a detective hat just like the one that Squirrelock Holmes wore. Dusty put that on right away and strutted around happily.

They also gave him a magnifying glass, a mirror to send signals, and some white gloves. The gloves were to be used so he wouldn't leave fingerprints when searching for clues. One thoughtful mole gave him a map of the entire Underground. Dusty had never felt more important in his whole life as he talked about his new job and trip.

During the refreshment time, no one seemed to notice that Musty left the party. She darted quickly out of the Town Hall and back home to pack her clothes. She had decided that she would go with Dusty on his journey.

In her room she packed her things and wrote a note to her parents. Then she slipped back to the party. She hadn't even been missed.

After the party Dusty's mother packed him a lunch for the trip. His father gave him a letter to give to Uncle Murky and the directions to his uncle's house. Then they all hugged Dusty good-bye. He would leave the next morning before any of them got up.

Musty wished she could say good-bye to her parents too, but her going must be kept secret. She gave them each an extra long good-night hug.

Before going to bed Dusty packed his knapsack. There just wasn't room for everything. Finally he decided to take his private eye sign, the letter for his uncle, the map, and the magnifying glass. Having finished his packing, he fell asleep and dreamed of working with Squirrelock and his uncle.

The next morning Musty heard Dusty's alarm go off. Dressing quietly, she opened her door and saw Dusty leave his room. She almost giggled out loud as she saw the private eye sign sticking out of his bundle. *That Dusty*, she thought. He probably forgot to bring his underwear, but he had to have that sign.

Musty waited just a few minutes to let him get a head start. Then she put the letter to her parents on her pillow and picked up her bundle. As she passed Dusty's room she noticed the mirror and other items still lying on his bed. She realized he hadn't had room for them. Thinking they would need them, she stopped and quickly stuffed them into her bundle.

When she left the burrow, Musty could hear Dusty's footsteps echoing through the tunnel. Staying just out of his sight, she followed him. A flutter of excitement swept over her. Where would all this lead them? Taking a deep breath, she hurried along following her brother.

STRANGER DANGER

Musty wondered if Dusty were heading in the right direction. There were so many twists and turns in the underground tunnel. Had he looked at his father's directions before he left?

As if in answer to her thought, Dusty stopped and opened the map of the Underground. Musty was careful to stay in the shadows and be very quiet. She wasn't yet ready for Dusty to know she was following him.

At last the boy mole put away the map. He had decided to take the left fork of the tunnel. After several miles of travel, he turned a sharp corner.

As Musty turned the corner, she heard voices ahead. She saw that Dusty was talking to someone he had met. Peering closer she saw that he was speaking to a sleazy looking shrew. She drew in her breath and wrinkled her nose. Shrews were ugly, mean animals and always a threat to moles.

"Good afternoon, my fine friend," said the slimy shrew in a slick voice. He was dressed well in a top hat and a long black coat with tails. A bow tie completed his costume, and he carried a wooden walking stick with a gold top. It was not his clothing, however, that annoyed Musty. She didn't like the way he was sidling up to Dusty.

He should be smart enough not to talk to strangers, thought Musty.

Mother Miranda Mole had often warned her little moles about such characters. Musty held her breath as she heard the shrew invite himself to walk along with Dusty. She saw her brother peering at the shrew through his glasses. He often did this when trying to make a decision.

Don't—oh, please don't, wished Musty.

But Dusty was saying, "Please feel free, Mr. Shrew. It would be nice to have your company."

Oh, no! fretted Musty. *He probably thinks this animal is all right because he's dressed so well. I wish he would be more careful when he's making new friends.*

Just then Musty felt a furry paw clamped across her mouth. "Don't make a sound," growled an animal. "If you do, you're in big trouble."

Musty tried her best to get free, but she couldn't. With great effort she managed to bring her tiny teeth down on the animal's paw.

The animal gave a scream of pain and dropped Musty with a thud. Scrambling quickly to get away, she saw the animal was another mole. She began to run wildly down the road in the direction they had come. However, Musty's short legs were no match for the larger mole's. In no time he caught her and yanked her off the road.

"Now stay put right there," he said roughly, shoving her down to the ground. Whipping a hanky from his pocket he tied it quickly around her mouth. "There!" he growled. "Now you won't sink your teeth in me again."

Musty watched fearfully as the mole looked at the wound where she had bitten him. She wished she had bitten him harder.

What does he want with me? she wondered in panic.
*Moles don't usually attack each other. Now I'm really
in a mess. I've lost sight of Dusty, and who knows what
will happen to me? Father and Mother were right. I should
never have come,* she thought gloomily, ready to cry.

MEET SAMMY SHREW

Meanwhile Dusty and the shrew walked along together chatting. After walking for some time, the shrew suggested they stop for lunch. Dusty agreed and, sitting down, opened his brown bag lunch that Mother Miranda had prepared for him. Taking a bite of his delicious earthworm sandwich, he politely offered a bite to the shrew.

The shrew shook his head. "I have something in this bag that's even better than an earthworm sandwich." Now Dusty loved earthworms so much he couldn't imagine what would be better. With curiosity he peered into the open bag the shrew held out to him.

"Achoo!" sneezed Dusty. "Achoo!" he sneezed again with tears streaming down his face. "Phew! What is that?" he asked, mopping his eyes and blowing his nose.

"This, my dear friend, is some of the most tender weeds your teeth will ever chew. Just smell it!"

Dusty poked his nose into the bag again and took a deep smell. Immediately he began to cough and sneeze and blow his nose.

"That stuff is pretty powerful. Are you sure it's just weeds?" he asked the shrew.

"Indeed, but of course you must learn to like it. I will give you a small amount for a sum of money. You see, these weeds are a very unusual mixture. They will give you the most wonderful feeling of happiness—"

"Mr. Shrew, I thank you for your kindness," interrupted Dusty, "but I must be highly allergic to your weeds. I wouldn't want to buy something that would make me ill."

"Oh, of course. I do understand. But surely just a little could not possibly harm you. It is something you need to get used to gradually. The treat is on me," coaxed the shrew, opening the bag again.

"Achoo!" sneezed Dusty. "Please put it away!"

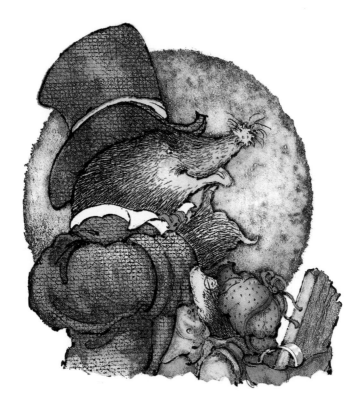

"As you like," said the shrew sadly. "If you won't buy some of my weeds, may I at least treat you to dinner this evening at my favorite restaurant, the Shrew's Stew? Their stew is particularly fine with dinner rolls and a turnip green salad."

"Why, yes, that would be nice," agreed Dusty, who was very fond of turnip greens anywhere or anytime. As he said that, he thought maybe he shouldn't take the time to go to the restaurant with the shrew. He needed to keep on his journey until he reached Uncle Murky's house. But he quickly put that thought from his mind. He wanted some turnip greens and meant to have some. He would worry about meeting Uncle Murky later.

THE SHREW'S STEW

Dusty walked quickly along beside the shrew, who appeared in a hurry to get to the Shrew's Stew. The sun was low in the sky when they finally came to a rundown building set back from the road.

The mole didn't like the looks of the restaurant. It had a dirty, seedy look, and some windows were boarded up so that no one could see in.

The boy mole wished he hadn't come. Surely turnip greens would not be very good in such a place.

The shrew pushed open the creaky door, and they entered a large damp room lit with only a few candles. Dusty could see several slouched forms of various animals—shrews, rabbits, a fox, and a couple of snakes. They were all sitting around tables with half-eaten food and bottles of drink in front of them. Most of them were sleeping at their tables.

The shrew guided Dusty to a small table close to the wall. Sitting down with him he tapped his cane on the floor, and a sloppy girl shrew shuffled up to their table to take their order.

"Yeah, whatcha want, Sammy?" she asked with a sneer.

"This dear friend of mine would like a nice order of turnip greens—right away—if you please."

Dusty looked around cautiously. He knew his father would not approve of this place. The animals at the other tables all looked very unhealthy, he thought. As his eyes adjusted to the light he saw an animal that looked like his sister.

Jumping to his feet he exclaimed, "That's my twin sister over there!" Dusty pointed to the table where Musty was sitting with another larger mole.

"Really?" said the shrew, looking where Dusty pointed.

"She's sitting with one of my men, Snarkey Mole. I wonder how she knows him? Has she been traveling with you?" he asked.

"No," said Dusty in a dazed way, sitting back down at the table. He was so stunned to see Musty he could hardly think straight. "She was at home in Molesbury with my parents when I left. I can hardly believe she is here."

"Well, let's get to the bottom of the mystery," said the shrew. Standing up, he motioned to the mole who was sitting with Musty. "Snarkey!" he yelled across the restaurant. "Bring your lady friend over here so I can meet her."

As Musty and Snarkey came over to his table the shrew said, "My dear, your brother is surprised to see you here. My name is Sammy Shrew, and I am most pleased to meet you."

"What are you doing here, Musty? I thought you were at home in Molesbury," exclaimed Dusty.

"Why, Dusty, you never know where I'm going to turn up." Musty laughed. "This is my friend Snarkey Mole."

"Pleased to meetcha," growled Snarkey.

He was sloppy looking and seemed to be very rude.

"Snarkey's one of my best men," said Sammy Shrew. "I'm sure he's showing you a good time, my dear." He gave Snarkey a sly wink.

"Oh yes, I'm having a wonderful time," she replied, slipping her paw through Snarkey's. "He's taking me sightseeing this evening."

Dusty felt sick all over at seeing his sister in such company. And she was acting so weird. Taking her by the paw he pulled her over closer to him. In a whisper he said, "What are you up to, Musty? You're not going anywhere with him."

"Oh, Dusty, you're too cute," simpered Musty in a silly way. "You can see I'm in good company." She giggled, looking up at Snarkey as they headed out the door.

"Musty!" called her brother urgently. "Wait! Father wouldn't want you to—"

But it was too late. Musty was already gone with Snarkey. Dusty felt a knot in the pit of his stomach. How could he help Uncle Murky when he had to worry about his sister?

6

ROSCOE

"Quite a little gal you have there," quipped the shrew, as Snarkey and Musty left the restaurant. "Don't worry about her, my boy. Snarkey knows his way around. Ah, here is your mess of turnip greens," he added, as the shrew waitress slammed the plate down on the table.

Dusty felt he couldn't eat a bite. How had Musty got here, and why was she acting so strangely? Did his parents know she was gone? And what about this Snarkey?

"Eat up, my fine friend. You don't always find such a fine serving of greens as these," Sammy said enthusiastically.

Dusty didn't want to be rude, so he sat down and began to eat the greens. Still chewing the last bite, he swallowed quickly and said, "I really must be going, Mr. Shrew. I have a long way to go before it is dark. Thank you so much for the good dinner."

Dusty darted through the door of the restaurant and looked both directions wildly. Which way had his sister and Snarkey gone?

Why does my silly sister have to horn in just now when I should be meeting Uncle Murky? I might as well go the way the directions show, he thought. Shoving his sleuth hat on his head, he started off in the direction of Uncle Murky's house.

The evening shadows loomed across the road as Dusty hurried along. *What will I do if I don't find her tonight?* he worried. He scurried along leaving a cloud of dust behind him. *I must find Musty before dark.*

To the left of the road he saw a mass of knotted roots. It looked like a good place to rest for a few minutes, so he sat down and wiped his face with his hanky.

Just then Dusty heard someone coming. Perhaps it was Musty! He could barely see the animal that was coming down the road in the twilight. As the animal drew closer he saw with disappointment that it was

only a rabbit. The hare approached Dusty and then spoke to him in a low whisper.

"You are Dusty Mole, aren't you?" he asked.

"Yes, I am," answered Dusty. "How do you know my name?"

"Shhh," warned the rabbit. Looking around in a secretive way, he answered, "Your Uncle Murky told me."

"Uncle Murky! I'm on my way to his house!"

"I know—and that is why I'm here. I'm Roscoe Rabbit, and I work with your Uncle Murky. You see, I haven't seen him for a week now, and I thought I should come by and tell you."

"My uncle sent for me to help him in his detective work," answered Dusty with concern. "If he's in trouble I want to do all I can to help him."

Roscoe looked at the little mole in a kind way. "The thing is, my friend, the whole Underground is puzzled. We just can't imagine what has happened to him."

Dusty felt the knot in his stomach tighten again. First the mess with Musty—and now his uncle was missing. *What next?* he wondered.

"Has anyone gone to see Squirrelock Holmes about it yet?" asked Dusty in a whisper. This would surely be a case for the great squirrel detective.

"Well, yes. You see, the Upstairs where Squirrelock lives has been spoiled by men who are selling a substance called drugs. These drugs, when used in a wrong way, cause sickness and death. The greedy men living Upstairs make a lot of money selling a drug called 'weed.' It causes you to feel really well and happy. But the happy feeling doesn't last.

"After people use the weed for a while, they want the happy feeling to continue. So they buy a stronger substance which causes great harm to their bodies.

"The stronger stuff gives such good feelings," continued Roscoe, "that the ones who take it get a craving for it. They want more and more of the stuff to continue their good feelings. They get hooked, which means they are addicts. They can't quit taking the strong drugs, even if they want to. Sometimes they are hooked for life."

Dusty could feel the fur standing up on the back of his neck, as it always did when danger was present. He shuddered.

"When people become addicts they must have their drugs every day or they get very ill," continued Roscoe, whispering. "So they will steal or even kill to get the money to buy the drugs, which are sold for very high prices. Even little children who live Upstairs have started taking the really bad substances.

"Squirrelock Holmes and your Uncle Murky are working hard to keep our animals from bringing the stuff below ground. It is dangerous work. Some of the moles from Molesbury have already been tricked into using the bad stuff. Why, just last week, a mole I know sold all his winter food to buy some of this weed. We must put a stop to these drug pushers," he added, with his bright eyes flashing.

Dusty looked at Roscoe with growing fear. Was that weed the shrew tried to sell him the bad stuff Roscoe was talking about? he wondered. Could Sammy Shrew be a drug pusher? Maybe Snarkey was one of those moles who had been tricked into using the stuff. If that were true, then Musty could be in real danger running around with him.

I've got to find her and Uncle Murky, thought Dusty.

THE WEED PUSHER

Dusty was shocked at Roscoe's news. "The weeds, Roscoe. That shrew tried to sell me weeds. Do you suppose—?"

"What shrew?" demanded Roscoe fiercely. "What are you talking about, and where did you see him?"

"Well, on the way here this morning I met Sammy Shrew."

"Sammy Shrew? Why he's the most notorious drug pusher and crook there is! Where did you see him?"

"I met him on the road, and he tried to sell me some weeds," answered Dusty. "I didn't buy any, but then he offered to take me to the Shrew's Stew. I probably shouldn't have gone, but I wanted some turnip greens they had."

"That Shrew's Stew is a bad place," observed Roscoe. "We think that it is being used by Sammy Shrew as a place to sell the bad substances. We can't actually catch him doing it though."

"I have another problem, Roscoe. While I was in the Shrew's Stew, I saw my twin sister, Musty. I don't know how she got there because she was at home in Molesbury when I left. I'm sure my parents don't know she's gone."

"Hmm," said Roscoe thoughtfully. "Are you sure it was she?"

"Oh, I'm sure all right. I talked to her. She was sitting with a creepy character, Snarkey Mole, and she left with him to go sightseeing. Sammy Shrew said Snarkey was one of his men. I'm really worried about my sister. I was just sitting here trying to decide whether to go on to Uncle Murky's or try to find her."

"Well, there's no use in going to your Uncle Murky's now. He isn't there. One of Squirrelock's agents is watching his house in case he comes home. He hasn't been there all week," replied Roscoe.

"Now that you've told me about the drugs and Sammy, I've just got to find Musty. I must get her out of here," said Dusty urgently.

"You're right," said the rabbit. "She isn't safe at all with Sammy Shrew around."

"Nor with this Snarkey Mole," agreed Dusty. "Do you know him?"

"I don't think so," admitted Roscoe. "But then I don't know many moles. I know more rabbits and squirrels, like Squirrelock and his agents."

"What do you think I should do?" asked Dusty.

"Well," said the rabbit thinking, "I imagine Snarkey and Musty will go back to the Shrew's Stew later tonight. Maybe you should go back there and wait for her. I'll find one of Squirrelock's agents to take her home."

"I can try," said Dusty doubtfully, "but she is very set in her ways. She doesn't always do what I want her to do."

"Well, you must try," said Roscoe. "While you're inside the Stew waiting for her, I'll contact Squirrelock. I'll ask for someone to take her safely through the Underground to Molesbury."

"OK," agreed Dusty. "Let's go!"

KIDNAPPED

The Shrew's Stew was even more crowded that night than it had been earlier in the day. The dimly lit room was filled with smoke that burned Dusty's eyes and made him wish for fresh air.

Making his way through the crowded tables, Dusty found a place back in the shadows and sat down to wait. Soon Snarkey and Musty came in, and Dusty motioned for them to join him at his table.

Musty saw him and yelled in a loud voice that seemed unlike her, "Hey, Snarkey, there's my brother, Dusty. Let's sit with him."

Snarkey and Musty sat down noisily. They ordered some food and began to eat. Musty looked at Dusty over her plate of stew and said, "I thought you were going to meet Uncle Murky. Have you seen him yet?"

Dusty looked at Musty with a warning to be quiet. He didn't want Snarkey or anyone in the restaurant to know he was connected with Uncle Murky.

But Musty didn't take the hint. "My brother is a private detective," she explained in a loud voice to Snarkey. "He's going to help our Uncle Murky with an important case."

Dusty frantically tried to signal Musty to be quiet, but she rattled on, seeming not to notice. Neither Dusty nor Musty noticed that Sammy Shrew and two foxes had come up behind them. Only Snarkey saw them coming.

Suddenly Dusty felt two strong paws clasp him and a low voice growled, "Get up slowly and come with us." Dusty jerked his head around as he was held captive by a fox on either side and Sammy Shrew behind. In a matter of seconds they roughly led Dusty away. Only

Musty and Snarkey were aware it was happening.

For a second Dusty looked at Musty and saw fear in her eyes. Musty's heart seemed to stop as she saw her brother taken away. She felt awful, knowing that she had led to his being captured.

Snarkey left the table and followed the animals as they led Dusty away. Musty was left alone at the table with her terrible fears. Looking around to be sure she wasn't being watched, she left the restaurant.

Moving quickly around
the corner of the Shrew's Stew,
Musty stayed in the shadows.
She was looking for some
clue as to where Dusty had
been taken. Roscoe had
not yet returned from
contacting Squirrelock,
so he didn't know anything
had happened to the two moles.

Where would they take him? wondered Musty
frantically. *I must find out and try to help him.* As she
darted along she thought how much she really cared
for her brother. She would feel terrible if something bad
happened to him.

Coming to the back of the restaurant, Musty saw
an old rundown cabin several feet away. It seemed a
likely place to look. Wiping a spot
clean on the filthy window, she saw
someone lying in a corner of the cabin.
Standing on her tiptoes and
straining to see, she thought
it was Dusty.

Just then a thick blanket was thrown over her head. "I've got her," growled a voice from the dark.

"You know what to do with her, don't you?" sneered the voice of Sammy Shrew. "These foolish moles walked right into our trap. Thought we wouldn't know they're part of Murky's gang. Ha! I knew the first time I met her foolish brother. That ridiculous Private Eye sign sticking out of his knapsack."

"Throw the little fool in the cabin with her precious brother. We'll get rid of these guys one by one if we have to."

Roughly the thugs carried the struggling Musty to the cabin and threw her inside. Then they locked the door. Musty untangled herself from the blanket and hurried over to her brother, who was still lying on the floor. *Is he alive?* she wondered.

Suddenly Molesbury seemed very far away to the frightened little mole. *Oh, why did we ever come on this awful trip?*

THE PIT

As she knelt beside her brother, he groaned and sat up. Musty gave a deep sigh of relief when she saw that Dusty was all right.

Looking around in a daze the boy mole asked, "Where am I? What happened?"

"It's OK, Dusty. We're in a cabin in back of the restaurant. They brought you here, and while I was looking for you, they grabbed me too. I guess they must have tried to knock you out."

Dusty jumped up, nearly knocking Musty over. He was madder than a wet hen! "Yeah, I guess they did," he retorted angrily. "I guess they wouldn't have, if you hadn't opened your mouth and blown my cover. How did you get here? What do you think you're doing messing around in a bad place like the Shrew's Stew?"

"Well—I—I—" began Musty.

"I can't believe you, Musty. You know Mom and Dad wouldn't want you to come!" continued Dusty in a loud voice. "I just knew you'd try to mess me up somehow. Where did you go this afternoon with that creep Snarkey?"

"He's not a creep, Dusty," answered Musty, lowering her voice.

"Not a creep?" yelled her brother. "Why Sammy Shrew himself said that he was one of his best men. How can you say he's not a creep?"

"Well—he—"

Just then a horrible sound filled the cabin.

"What's that?" asked Musty fearfully. She jumped over closer to her brother.

There it was again! "Oooaaaah! Oaauuuh!"

"I don't know," admitted Dusty, whose every hair was standing straight up in fear. "Be quiet!" he warned as the horrible sound came again. It sounded ghostly! "Maybe someone fell down in the cellar and is injured," he whispered.

"Or—or—was—thr—thrown down there," stuttered his sister, who could hardly speak. Her teeth were chattering in fear. "It's so dark—I c—can't see a th—thing."

"Maybe we don't want to see," the boy mole said seriously. "Take my paw, Musty, and follow me. We've got to find out what it is."

Musty clutched Dusty's paw tightly, gulping down her fear that threatened to make her sick.

"Ooaah!" the terrible sound continued.

"Musty! I think this is a trap door," cried Dusty, feeling around the floor in the dark. The two moles groped until Dusty found another board that gave way as he pried on it. A small trap door opened to an even darker cellar below the cabin floor. As they opened the door the sound grew louder. Whatever was making the noise was down there!

"Close it up, Dusty!" cried the girl mole. "We can sit on the door and keep it down there!"

"We can't do that, Musty!" said her twin with disgust. Girls were such fraidy-cats! "We've gotta check it out."

"You—you mean go d—down there?" asked Musty in unbelief.

"Yeah. I'll go, and you stay here. If I need you, I'll yell," he said with a bravery he didn't feel.

Musty didn't like the prospect of staying up in the cabin alone. She liked even less the thought of going down into the black pit. As she watched, Dusty began to descend into the hole. Musty peered after him. Her heart pounded. What if he never came up out of the hole? What would she do?

"Are you all right, Dusty?" she whispered fearfully, as he disappeared into the hole. "Have you found anything?" The groaning sounds continued all the while.

"Yeah, I've found something," called her twin. "It's a half-dead animal of some kind. I'll bring it up if I can, but I may need your help. Do you think you can get down here?"

Musty gulped. "S—sure," she called in a quavery voice, beginning to climb down into the pit.

Dusty talked to her encouragingly until she reached the floor of the pit. The blackness was so thick she couldn't even see him.

"Over here," he called. She made her way toward his voice. "This poor fellow is really in bad shape," said Dusty. "I'm afraid he's almost gone, but let's try to drag him up where we can see better."

Together the moles tugged at their heavy burden, pulling him up with them an inch at a time. The animal's groans were heart-wrenching. Sometimes they feared he would die before they got him up into the cabin.

After what seemed hours, they pushed their heavy burden through the trap door. Then they fell into an exhausted heap beside him. They could help him no further until they had rest.

JUNIOR AGENT

Finally the murky morning light began to filter through the dirty windows of the cabin. Musty woke up and looked around. The animal they had rescued stirred and groaned.

Musty shuddered and looked at the animal closer. She stared in unbelief. *I think I recognize that sweater!* she thought. She could hardly believe her eyes. *It's Uncle Murky!*

"Dusty!" she screamed. "It's Uncle Murky! Hurry! Wake up! He's still alive!"

Dusty sat up sleepily, rubbing his eyes. When he saw Uncle Murky, Dusty woke up instantly and knelt beside his injured uncle.

"He's still alive, isn't he?" asked Musty with excitement. There were tears in her eyes as she saw how sick and injured her favorite uncle was.

"Barely," answered Dusty. "They must have beaten and drugged him!" He put his uncle's head in his lap and tried to make him more comfortable. "He needs help badly, or he'll die. We've got to get out of here," he said.

"You're right," said Musty, hopping up. "I think Snarkey should be watching now." She searched through her pockets.

"Snarkey! What does that creep have to do with it?"

"I was trying to tell you when we heard Uncle Murky groaning," said Musty, still digging through her pockets. "Here it is," she cried happily, pulling out a mirror.

"Musty, be real! Here is Uncle Murky ready to die, and you're looking for a mirror to primp. Just like a silly girl," he snorted with disgust.

Musty seemed not to notice what Dusty said. She pulled a very small notebook out of her other pocket.

"Hey! That's the decoding notebook Uncle Murky sent me. Where did you get that?" he demanded.

"You left it behind, Dusty. You didn't have room to bring it because you brought that silly Private Eye sign. I brought it along when I decided to follow you."

"I didn't know you were following me. I—"

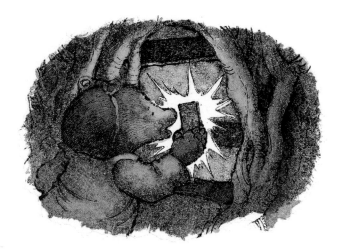

But Musty wasn't listening. She ran to the window and wiped a spot clean. Then she began moving the mirror back and forth, catching the light from the tunnel torches.

"Wait a minute, Musty. Who are you signaling? Give me that mirror," said Dusty struggling to get up.

Uncle Murky, who was still lying with his head in Dusty's lap, started to groan again. Dusty settled back in frustration, not wanting to disturb his uncle.

Musty continued at the window, answering, "I'm sending signals to Snarkey. He said he'd be watching."

"I bet he will," scoffed Dusty, "and he'll let Sammy Shrew take care of us. You're such a silly little fool, Musty. You're just getting us in more trouble."

Suddenly the door burst open. There was Sammy
Shrew and the two foxes.

"Think you can get away with sending signals?"
Sammy leered. "We'll teach you two a lesson. Let 'em
have it, guys. Get the old guy, too!"

The two foxes came slowly toward them. Musty
gasped with fear. There was no escape now.

Just then it seemed an explosion hit the cabin. The door burst open, and Snarkey Mole, Roscoe, and Squirrelock's agents swarmed in.

"Stand where you are! Don't move a muscle!" growled Snarkey Mole. He grabbed Sammy Shrew and pinned his paws behind him. "Get the foxes, men!" he cried, and the agents captured the deadly foxes.

"You won't get away with this, Snarkey," screamed the shrew. "My men have this place covered."

"You don't have any men now, Sammy. They've all been rounded up by the police. This will be the last of the Shrew's Stew and your terrible business of drug pushing," stated Snarkey.

"I might have known. Running a double racket, were you, Snarkey?" snorted Sammy with disgust. "I never should have trusted you."

Dusty watched in amazement. He could hardly believe his eyes. "What is—Snarkey? You aren't working for Sammy Shrew?"

"Snarkey is an undercover agent," explained Musty. "He snatched me on the road here. I bit him and tried to get away, but he gagged me and made me listen to him. He wanted me to help him find Uncle Murky.

That's why I was acting so funny. I wanted them to think I was one of them, too. He said the only way we could find Uncle Murky would be for one of us to be captured. He figured they'd throw us in with him, and then he'd know where he was."

"We weren't sure where they were holding him," added Snarkey. "I knew it was somewhere here at the restaurant, but I wasn't sure where."

"I should have fixed you long ago, Snarkey," snarled Sammy.

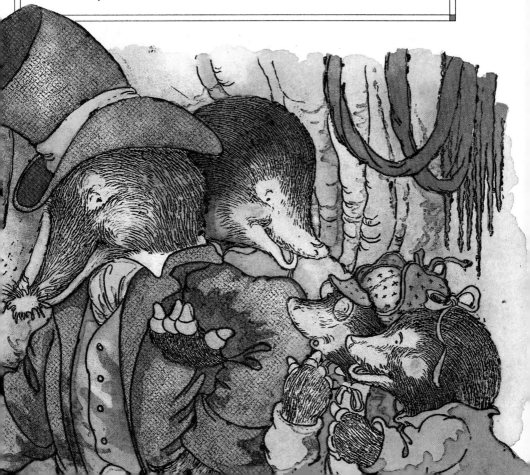

"Well, you won't be fixing anyone again," said a deep voice of authority. All eyes in the room turned toward the door as Squirrelock Holmes entered. "Take them away, men," he commanded.

His agents removed the snarling shrew and foxes.

Musty shuddered as they left. She felt so much better once they were gone.

"How's my old pal Murky?" asked Squirrelock with concern. He came over to where Dusty still sat with Uncle Murky. "I think he's coming around, sir," Dusty responded. "They had him in a pit under the cabin. He's in pretty bad shape." Dusty looked with awe at his hero, the great squirrel detective, now kneeling by his uncle.

"Hmm, probably drugged. He'll be all right if we get him to a hospital. That leg is broken and will need attention." Beckoning to some of his men who were standing by, he helped Dusty get his uncle situated on a stretcher.

Uncle Murky opened his eyes and said weakly, "Hello, Squirrelock. I haven't done too well, have I?"

"You've done very well, old friend," responded the squirrel detective. "And so have your nephew and niece." He motioned for them to come over so they could talk to Uncle Murky.

"Dusty!" cried Uncle Murky with pleasure. "I knew you'd be a help—but what is my little niece Musty doing here? I didn't expect her to come."

"Musty saved the day for us, Uncle Murky. She brought along the mirror and code notebook and was working with Snarkey Mole all along," said Dusty proudly. "I didn't know he was an undercover agent."

"You were quite wonderful, my dear," said Squirrelock to Musty. "It was very dangerous, but we were watching you constantly. We would have moved in sooner if we'd thought you were in too much danger."

Squirrelock's men took Murky away then, so that he could receive medical attention. Dusty and Musty promised to follow with the squirrel detective.

"I've been in touch with your parents this morning, Musty," said Squirrelock. "You should never have left without their permission, you know," he rebuked gently. "They have been so worried about you. I'm afraid you will have some correction to face at home when you return."

Musty dropped her head, and tears filled her eyes. "I feel bad about that now," said the girl mole. "I'll never leave home without permission again."

"That is fine, my dear. And things worked out very well this time," he responded.

"I'm surely glad she came, sir," said Dusty humbly. "I don't know what I'd have done without my sister." He put his paw on her shoulder.

Musty felt her spirits lift. Although she must still face her disappointed and worried parents, Uncle Murky was all right, and Dusty was glad she had come.

"Hey, Squirrelock, what should I do with this sign I found?" asked one of the detective's agents. He was carrying Dusty's Private Eye sign.

"Uh, you can just throw it away," said Dusty quickly, with a bit of shame in his voice.

"But, Dusty, won't you need it when you get home?" asked Musty.

"No, I don't think so, Musty. I've learned there's a lot more to being a private eye than I thought. I think I'll make a new sign that will say DUSTY AND MUSTY MOLE, JUNIOR AGENTS. Would you like that, sis?" he asked.

"I sure would," cried Musty excitedly. "Let's go, partner," she added happily, linking her paw with her brother's.

Squirrelock, Roscoe, and Snarkey laughed and followed the happy moles out of the cabin. They were on their way to the next Molehole Mystery adventure.

THROUGH THE SPYGLASS

Wouldn't it be fun if we could look in on Dusty and Musty and see what happens next? Well, keep reading through my spyglass and let's see what's in their future.

The two little moles stayed with Uncle Murky for a while until he felt well enough to go back to work. Musty cooked good meals and kept house for them. When Uncle Murky was well, Squirrelock offered him a new job as head of all his agencies.

Dusty and Musty returned to Molesbury and were awarded a citation for their great work in cracking the drug ring. On the day they received their award Dusty praised his sister, Musty, for her help.

He told the story of her having the mirror and notebook, and how her undercover work with Snarkey Mole had saved the day.

Junior Agent Dusty was invited to speak about drugs to the students at the Molesbury school. He told how the upstairs was being spoiled by men who sold these drugs and how sometimes even children would experiment with them and get hooked for life. He challenged all his friends in Molesbury to stay away from drugs that are harmful, so they could have a healthy and successful life.

Dusty and Musty formed a club called the Molehole Mystery Club. This club was fun because they worked on other mysteries and had many adventures. It became well known in Molesbury as a club that helped kids stay away from drugs.

UNDERGROUND
"DIG-TIONARY"

MOLE (mōl): A burrowing animal that spends most of its life underground *(Webster's New Collegiate Dictionary)*.

Have you ever seen a molehill? It is a low ridge of dirt sometimes seen in fields, lawns, or gardens. Such ridges are made by moles as they search for earthworms and grubs for food. The tunnel, where the moles live, is a place of safety from other animals who would harm them.

The Lord has created the moles' front feet to be used as rigid shovels for digging. The back feet are used for bracing themselves as they dig. As much as ten pounds of soil may be shoveled in twenty minutes. This remarkable amount is about fifty times the weight of the mole.

In the summer, moles burrow close to the surface to feed on their favorite food, earthworms. In the winter, they must dig their tunnels and burrows much deeper to find the worms, who have dug farther underground to find protection from the cold.

Did you know that moles' eyes are really narrow slits covered with fur? Although their eyes are small, moles are not really blind. God has equipped them with all they need to live and find their food.

Most of us have never held a mole. If we did, we would be surprised to find it very small. Usually moles are never more than six inches long, and they weigh less than four ounces.

Moles are often said to be "mysterious," because they are difficult to find and observe. Their most useful purpose is to break up the ground and provide oxygen for the soil.

They are sometimes called the "farmer's pest" because of their unwelcome ridges and burrows. Nevertheless, moles are one of God's special creations and fulfill the purpose for which He created them.

JOIN
MOLEHOLE MYSTERY
CLUB

Would you like to join the Molehole Mystery Club? This will entitle you to receive your very own Molehole Mystery Club ID card and Dusty's free newsletter. The newsletter will be filled with clues and mysteries you can solve and lots of fun things to do.

The newsletter will share things with you from God's Word that will help you live a happy life as a child of God. My spyglass shows me some wonderful words from the Bible that you need to remember always.

These verses are the Molehole Mystery Club Motto, and you will need to memorize them to become a member. The words are found in the Bible [1 Thessalonians 5:21 and 22]: "Test everything. Hold on to the good. Avoid [stay away from] every kind of evil" *(New International Version)*.

We'll be looking for your membership application for our club. See you in the next Molehole adventure story. Happy reading!